MySELF Bookshelf

The Drummer Boy

By SooHyeon Min
Illustrated by Peggy Nille
Language Arts Consultant: Joy Cowley

NORWOOD HOUSE PRESS
Chicago, Illinois

DEAR CAREGIVER

MySELF ▊▐▊ **Bookshelf** is a series of books that support children's social emotional learning. SEL has been proven to promote not only the development of self-awareness, responsibility, and positive relationships, but also academic achievement.

Current research reveals that the part of the brain that manages emotion is directly connected to the part of the brain that is used in cognitive tasks, such as: problem solving, logic, reasoning, and critical thinking—all of which are at the heart of learning.

SEL is also directly linked to what are referred to as 21st Century Skills: collaboration, communication, creativity, and critical thinking. MySELF Bookshelf offers an early start that will help children build the competencies for success in school and life.

In these delightful books, young children practice early reading skills while learning how to manage their own feelings and how to be considerate of other perspectives. Each book focuses on aspects of SEL that help children develop social competence that will benefit them in their relationships with others as well as in their school success. The charming characters in the stories model positive traits such as: responsibility, goal setting, determination, patience, and celebrating differences. At the end of each story, you will find a letter that highlights the positive traits and an activity or discussion to help your child apply SEL to his or her own life.

Above all, the most important part of the reading experience is to have fun and enjoy it!

Sincerely,

Shannon Cannon

Shannon Cannon, Ph.D.
Literacy and SEL Consultant

Norwood House Press • P.O. Box 316598 • Chicago, Illinois 60631
For more information about Norwood House Press please visit our website at www.norwoodhousepress.com or call 866-565-2900.

Shannon Cannon – Literacy and SEL Consultant
Joy Cowley – English Language Arts Consultant
Mary Lindeen – Consulting Editor

Library of Congress Cataloging-in-Publication Data
Min, SooHyeon.
The drummer boy / by SooHyeon Min ; illustrated by Peggy Nille.
pages cm. -- (MySelf bookshelf)
Summary: "Rukundo is known in his village as a drummer. He is devastated when his family falls ill with cholera after drinking dirty water. Rukundo plays his drum as reporters write an article about him. When the article is published showing Rukundo as the Little Drummer Boy, several people read the story and buy the village a water pump"-- Provided by publisher.
ISBN 978-1-59953-661-3 (library edition : alk. paper) -- ISBN 978-1-60357-721-2 (ebook)
[1. Water supply--Fiction. 2. Drum--Fiction. 3. Social action--Fiction. 4. Blacks--Rwanda--Fiction. 5. Rwanda--Fiction.] I. Nille, Peggy, 1972- illustrator. II. Title.
PZ7.1.M63Dr 2015
[E]--dc23
                                        2014030344

Manufactured in the United States of America in Stevens Point, Wisconsin.
263N—122014

The Drummer Boy

Rukundo lived in Rwanda, Africa.
He was a very good drummer.
Boom-boom! Boom-boom!
The sound of his drum
woke people in the morning.
The drum told everyone that
a new day had begun.

4

6

Rukundo's mother said,
"Rukundo, hurry! Get some water."

Grabbing two plastic containers,
Rukundo set off on the dirt road.
Other children were running
with containers in their hands.
They could go to school
after they had brought water
back to their village.

8

Rukundo was first at the watering hole.
The water was dirty, but even dirty water
was hard to find in Rwanda.

He filled the containers with a cup.
One, two, three, four, five, six…
After a while the yellow containers
were filled.

It was a long walk to the watering hole
and a long walk back home again.
Rukundo wanted to make a lot of money
so he could put a water pump in his village.
He had heard there was good clean water
under the hard dry ground.
If only it could be pumped up!
He was happy with the thought
that he could be the one
who bought a water pump for his people.

Rukundo gave water to his brother and sisters.
When they drank water from the watering hole,
they often got stomach aches.
But they could not live without water.

"Mother," he said, "can I go to school now?"

His mother sighed. "I'm sorry, Rukundo.
They have a fever and need more to drink.
You have to go to the watering hole again."

Rukundo had not been to school for days.
If he hurried, he could make the last class.
He ran with the full water containers
but he tripped over a stone.
Water poured out into the dirt.
His knee was skinned and bleeding.
"I am a fool." he said.

The sun was setting
when he limped into the village.
But no one was at home.
A neighbor called to him.
"Rukundo, your brother and sisters
are very sick in the hospital.
Your mother is with them."

16

Rukundo forgot about his sore knee.
He ran to the hospital,
still carrying his containers.

17

His brother and sisters were in beds
in the old hospital tent.
His mother said in a weary voice,
"The doctor said they have cholera
from drinking dirty water.
Many children are sick with cholera.
Some have even died."

Rukundo poured the water
out of the containers.
If only they had a water pump!

19

Rukundo was very angry
that the dirty water
had made his family sick.
He did not know what to do.
He started to beat
the empty yellow container.
Boom-boom! Boom-boom!
Tears fell on the plastic drum.

Click! Click!
A man was taking pictures
of the drummer boy.

Stories were written about
Rukundo and the dirty water.

Little Drummer Boy in Rwanda!

Rukundo's Yellow Container!

Help!
Give Hope to Rukundo
and the Children of Rwanda!

Clean Water for Rwanda's Children!

One Water Pump
Saves Thousands of Children!

23

One year passed,
and the small village
was full of happiness.
Some good-hearted people
had read the story of Rukundo,
and they had installed a water pump
in Rukundo's village.

Rukundo was allowed to pump first.
As the sparkling water gushed out,
everyone cheered and shouted,
"Hooray, little drummer boy!"

25

Now Rukundo travels around the world.
He does not beat his drum in anger.
He beats it with hope for the children
in Africa who still do not have clean water.

Wherever Rukundo beats his drum,
more people will learn about Africa,
and then more children will be saved.

Boom-boom! Boom-boom! Boom-boom!

Dear Readers,

I am very glad to tell you the story of Rukundo and his yellow plastic drum. Many things happen in the world. Some are sad things, like poverty and drought. It is hard to live without money and clean water.

Many people in Africa and other places in the world live like this every day. When we hear about these people, we feel bad for them. We may think there is nothing we can do to help.

But there are people like Rukundo who awaken the love in our hearts. They tell us how we can help. Together, we can make the world a better place.

Sincerely,
The Author

SOCIAL AND EMOTIONAL LEARNING FOCUS

Social Responsibility

Rukundo is a boy who used his talent to make a difference for all the people in his village. Instead of raising money to buy himself toys, or even a new drum, Rukundo put other people's needs before his own. Rukundo teaches us that kids can make a difference in the world by helping others.

Maybe you and your friends would like to work together to create a campaign for a cause that is important to you. To campaign means to work in an organized and active way to reach a goal—usually a social one. A social goal is something that will help others or make people aware of challenges. Not all campaigns raise money, some raise awareness by educating people about the challenges other people face.

Decide on a cause that is important to you. Visit this website to get ideas about how children all over the world campaigned to make a difference:

http://www.kidscanmakeadifference.org/what-kids-can-do

After you have decided on your cause. Make a plan. Here are some ideas to get you started:

1. Develop a Timeline

When will your campaign begin and end? Is this based on dates, or on the amount of money you hope to raise, or number of people you hope to reach?

2. Do the Research

Find information to help educate your audience about your cause. Who does it affect? What can be done to help?

3. Create your message

The message should answer the question, "Why should people care about this?" The message should let people know what you want them to do to support your cause.

(continued on next page)

4. Assign Jobs

Everyone on the team should contribute. Whether it's making things to sell and raise money, speaking about your cause in public, writing a blog, or designing posters and fliers to distribute, each person can use his or her talents to support the campaign.

5. Get the Word Out

Advertise your campaign. You can make posters and fliers, or use social media.

6. Keep Track of Your Progress

Every week, look at the progress you have made toward your goal. If you are raising money, keep track of how much you have raised. If you are raising awareness, keep track of the number of people or ways you have reached people to educate them about your cause.

7. Share Your Success

Be sure to tell people about your progress in reaching your goal. You might even get a local newspaper or television station to report on your efforts.

Reader's Theater

Reader's Theater is an interactive approach to reading that allows students to understand each story through dramatic interpretation. By involving students in reading, listening, and speaking activities, they provide an integrated approach for students to develop fluency and comprehension. A Reader's Theater edition of this book is available online. You can access the script by scanning the QR code to the right or visit our website at: http://www.norwoodhousepress.com/drummerboy.aspx